I'm a Frog!

To Trixie,
and her abundant imagination

ISBN 978-1-338-21368-3

12 11 10 9 8 7 6 5   18 19 20 21 22

Printed in the U.S.A.   40

First Scholastic printing, September 2017

An ELEPHANT & PIGGIE Book   SCHOLASTIC INC.

Ribbit!

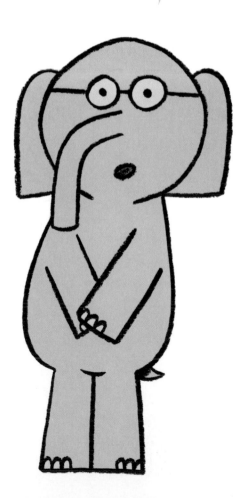

I was sure
you were a pig.

You look like a pig.

And your name *is* "Piggie."

15

17

About five minutes ago.

20

21

24

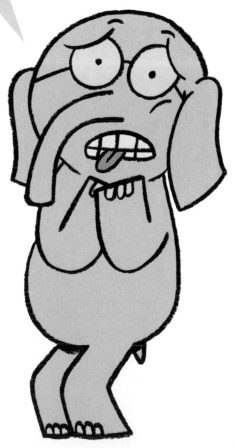

I DO NOT
TO BE A

29

32

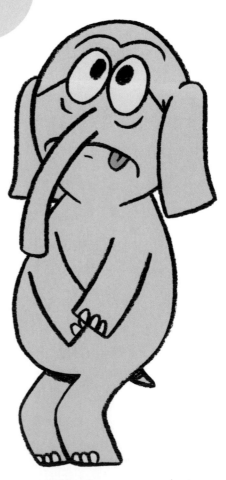

Pretending is when you act like something you are not.

40

All the time.

47

No, I can't!

Yes, you can!

No, I can't!

No, I can't!

Yes, you can!

No, I can't!

No, I can't!

Yes, you can!

52

Why can't you
pretend to be
a frog!?

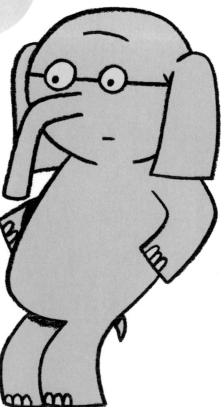

Because I am a cow.

End!

Have you read all of Elephant and Piggie's funny adventures?

Today I Will Fly!

My Friend Is Sad

I Am Invited to a Party!

There Is a Bird on Your Head!
(Theodor Seuss Geisel Medal)

I Love My New Toy!

I Will Surprise My Friend!

Are You Ready to Play Outside?
(Theodor Seuss Geisel Medal)

Watch Me Throw the Ball!

Elephants Cannot Dance!

Pigs Make Me Sneeze!

I Am Going!

Can I Play Too?

We Are in a Book!
(Theodor Seuss Geisel Honor)

I Broke My Trunk!
(Theodor Seuss Geisel Honor)

Should I Share My Ice Cream?

Happy Pig Day!

Listen to My Trumpet!

Let's Go for a Drive!
(Theodor Seuss Geisel Honor)

A Big Guy Took My Ball!
(Theodor Seuss Geisel Honor)

I'm a Frog!

My New Friend Is So Fun!

Waiting Is Not Easy!
(Theodor Seuss Geisel Honor)

I Will Take a Nap!

I *Really* Like Slop!

The Thank You Book

Gerald is careful. Piggie is not.
Piggie cannot help smiling. Gerald can.
Gerald worries so that Piggie does not have to.

Gerald and Piggie are best friends.

In *I'm a Frog!* Piggie has some *ribbiting* news! Can Gerald make the leap required to accept Piggie's new identity?

★"These masterful mini-dramas will delight and amuse easy-reader and picture-book audiences, alike."
—*School Library Journal* (starred review)

★"These books will easily take their place alongside Seuss and Eastman as classics in the beginning-reader genre."
—*The Bulletin* (starred review)

Mo Willems,

a number one *New York Times* best-selling author and illustrator, has been awarded a Caldecott Honor on three occasions, for *Don't Let the Pigeon Drive the Bus!*, *Knuffle Bunny: A Cautionary Tale*, and *Knuffle Bunny Too: A Case of Mistaken Identity*. Other favorites include *Leonardo, the Terrible Monster* and *The Story of Diva and Flea*.

Mo began his career as a writer and animator on *Sesame Street*, where he garnered six Emmy Awards. He lives with his family in Massachusetts.

This edition is available for distribution only through the school market.
Cover art © 2013 by Mo Willems

■ SCHOLAST

www.scholastic.c

ISBN 978-1-338-21368-3

EAN

9 781338 213683

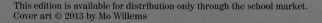

Don't miss **Let's Go for a Drive!**; **A Big Guy Took My Ball!**; and all the other Elephant & Piggie books!